SQUAWKY

The Little Blue Jay

To: Isaac

Melissa Jones

Todd A. Jones

MELISSA A. JONES

www.trafford.com

North America & international
toll-free: 1 888 232 4444 (USA & Canada)
fax: 812 355 4082

Dedication

This book is dedicated to my father-in-law Alfred C. Jones,
who told me "there is a book in all of us." This inspired me
to put my thoughts into words so that others might enjoy
it. And to my husband Todd, who believed in me, supported
me and helped me in the editing portion of the text.

If just one child or adult gets joy from this book,
then I will be happy that it was published.

I was born in Salem, Oregon in 1960, and raised in the small town
of Independence, OR. I met my husband in 1978, and we were
married in 1981. We have two daughters and 3 grand daughters.

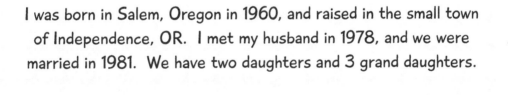

Sally will always remember that special day. It was a beautiful spring morning, the sun was shining brightly, and the birds were chirping.

"Sally," her father called for her. "Come outside with me. I will push you on the swing."

"Higher, Daddy, push me higher."

As Sally was swinging, she noticed a very pretty bird in the tree.

"Daddy, look at that blue bird in that tree," she said, pointing to the tree on the other side of the yard.

"That's a blue jay," her dad told her.

As Sally and her dad were looking at the blue jay, another one flew up with a twig in its mouth.

"I think those blue jays are building a nest in that tree," said Sally's dad.

1

Sally jumped from the swing, excited that the birds were making a nest in her yard. She stood beneath the tree, looking up.

"Hi, pretty birds," she called up to them.

The birds turned around, looking down at her. They chirped very loudly, as if to say something to her.

"What are they saying to me, Daddy?"

"I don't understand bird talk, honey," her father said. "Come on now, Sally, it's time for us to get some lunch."

"Bye, birdies," she shouted to them.

"I'm going to visit you every day."

"Come on, Sally" her father said, smiling.

Every day after school, the first thing Sally did was run to the backyard to see the blue jays in the tree. She always talked to them.

"Hi, birdies," she called up to the happy family. The birds always talked back to her. "Chirp, chirp, chirp."

"I wish I knew what you were saying to me," Sally would say with a wrinkled brow.

Sometimes, Sally would sit in her swing, looking at the happy birds. She just loved her new feathered friends.

"I'm so glad you picked my yard to build your nest in."

Sally was happy, swinging and singing to the birds. "La, la la, la, la."

She really cared about her birdie pals!

Then one day it happened! Sally ran to the backyard after school and discovered that mother bird's eggs had hatched!

"Daddy, Daddy!" she screeched, running into the house to get him. "Look, look! There are baby birdies up in the nest," she gasped.

Little Sally loved having a nest of baby birds in her yard. It made her feel special that they picked her house to build their nest. She would talk to them and sing to them and listen to their little chirping. She wished they could understand her, and she wished that she could understand them.

The baby birds seemed to be growing very fast. Sally would talk to them every day. The birds would talk back to her. One of the babies was very loud.

"Squawk!" it would yell at her.

"You're sure a noisy one!" she said, pointing to one of the babies. "I'm going to name you Squawky."

"And don't you worry, I won't ever hurt you," Sally would reassure them.

The babies were getting bigger and had begun jumping all around in the tree, wanting to learn to fly. One day one jumped on a branch very close to where Sally was sitting under the tree. The mother bird started flapping her wings wildly and squawking at her baby.

"Don't go near people," the mother bird scolded her baby bird. "They could hurt you."

The baby bird jumped into the nest. Mother bird squawked loudly at her baby. "Don't get near humans. They are mean. Stay away from all people," she said with anger.

Sally loved sitting in her swing, watching the mother and father bird caring for their baby birds. They would take worms and bugs to them.

Sally would sing and talk to them, hoping they understood her.

"Hi, birdies, I love you," she would say.

They would just look at her with their little heads cocked to the side, wondering what those noises were coming from her mouth.

One day Squawky was looking down at Sally in her swing. She was singing and reading a book to the birds.

Squawky asked his mom, "What is she saying to me, Mommy?"

"I don't know, tweetie pie. I don't understand people talk."

Sally and her dad would often go out to swing and play in the backyard. They would look up and talk to the birds.

"Hi. How are you today?" she would ask them.

Squawky asked his mom, "Why can't we understand her? She seems so nice."

"I don't know, but stay away from them," she would warn.

One morning Squawky was playing in the tree with his brother bird, when suddenly he slipped off a branch and fell to a lower branch. His wing was caught! Poor Squawky was hanging helplessly upside down, twelve feet off the ground. He cried loudly for his mother and father to help him. As brother bird watched intently, the parents both tried to lift him up. They tried to pull on him. They tried everything in their power to help him, but they just couldn't free him from the tree's grasp.

Squawky tried to free himself, but it was hopeless. His mother and father watched and worried as Squawky weakened. But they could not help him. They wished so much that they could save him, but he was stuck. Really stuck!

When Sally got home from school that day, she went to the tree as usual to greet her bird friends. She was shocked at what she saw when she looked up. There, hanging lifelessly in the tree by one wing, was her little Squawky.

Sally ran into the house, horrified at what she had just seen.

"The phone, I've got to get to the phone and call Daddy at work!"

The phone seemed to ring forever. When her father finally answered, Sally yelled into the phone, "Daddy, Daddy, hurry home! Squawky is caught in the tree. I think he might be dead!"

"Slow down!" said Sally's dad. "Honey, take a deep breath and tell me what happened."

Sally tried to calm herself. "I came home to find Squawky hanging by one wing in the tree."

Knowing how much the birds in the tree meant to his little girl, her dad said, "I'll be home as soon as I can, sweetheart."

22

"But Daddy, you have to come home now. Squawky needs help. He's way up in the tree too."

"Okay," replied Dad. "I'll be home in a few minutes."

When Sally's dad arrived home, Sally was crying and waiting in the driveway.

"Hurry, Daddy, hurry!" Sally yelled to her dad. "He's this way," she cried, pointing to the backyard.

Sally and her dad ran through the gate to the backyard.

When Sally's dad looked up at Squawky hanging limply in the tree, he was sure that he didn't make it there in time to save the little bird.

He hurried to the garage to get the ladder. Sally helped him carry it to the backyard.

Sally's dad placed the ladder against the tree.

"Hold the ladder, Sally, while I climb up to see if I can reach Squawky."

As he got closer to Squawky, he saw his little feet move.

"I think he's still alive, Sally!" he yelled down to her.

"Oh, please be alive, Squawky!" she whispered hopefully.

Squawky's family was high up in the branches, looking down.

They were very concerned about the human getting so close to their baby.

The ladder was not quite long enough, so Sally's dad had to climb up into the tree above the end of the ladder. Gently, he was able to grab the young Squawky and lift him up until he was free.

But Squawky was limp and lifeless.

Squawky's parents chirped loudly at Sally's dad, wondering what was going to become of their baby. They were sure that was the last they would ever see of their sweet little guy.

29

The poor little blue jay had been stuck in the tree for some time without food or water.

"I'm going to find a shoebox to put him in, Daddy. Then I will pad it with some soft cloth. Do you think he can drink water from an eyedropper?" Sally asked her dad.

"I don't know if he is strong enough for that, honey, but we can try," he said, not really believing that Squawky would survive.

Squawky's family was sure he was gone forever. But what they didn't know was that Sally and her dad were trying everything they can to bring Squawky back to life.

That night, Sally and her dad were finally able to give the baby bird some water.

"Daddy, do you think he's going to live?" Sally wondered.

"It's hard to tell at this point. We'll just have to check on him in the morning, honey. Speaking of which, you had better be getting into bed. It's late."

"Okay, Daddy, good night. I love you."

The next morning, Sally jumped out of bed before her alarm went off. Down the stairs she ran, anxious and hopeful.

"Daddy, Daddy, wake up, wake up!"

"What is it, Sally, what's wrong?" gasped her sleepy father.

"Squawky is still alive!" Sally shouted excitedly.

Still not moving around much, he looked very weak, but the little bird seemed more alert. Sally and her dad decided to try to feed him. After Sally collected some worms from the garden, her dad ground them up and added a little water so they could put the wormy mixture in an eyedropper.

"Do you think he will eat it, Daddy?" Sally asked.

"All we can do is try," he replied.

Well, Squawky didn't eat just a little bit. He ate a lot!

For two days the humans fed the little bird worms and bugs from the eyedropper. Squawky seemed to be getting stronger every day.

Meanwhile, Squawky's family was very sad and missed him very much, but the mother and father blue jay still must work hard to feed the rapidly growing baby birds left in the nest.

On the third day, Squawky's mother was in search of food. As she flew past Sally's kitchen window, she thought she heard a familiar squawk.

"No, it couldn't be," she thought as she screeched to a halt and landed on a branch not far from the window.

"Squawk, squawk!" came the sound from inside the house.

Sure enough, to the mother's surprise, inside the humans' house was her baby bird. She chirped at him, and he chirped back to her, "I'm okay, Mommy!"

Squawky's mother was so happy she forgot all about getting food. Instead she flew right back to the nest and told her family, "Our baby is still alive!"

The next morning Sally got up to take care of Squawky as usual.
But this was not to be a usual day.

"Daddy, Daddy, Daddy! Squawky is gone!"

Sally's dad came into the kitchen and peered into the
empty shoebox.

"He has to be here somewhere, Sally. Let's start looking for the
little guy."

"Sally! Look! Here's Squawky! He's on the lampshade by
the window!"

"Sally, you know what I think?"

"I know, Daddy. We have to put Squawky back in the nest, don't we?" she said sadly.

"Yes, dear. But we should be happy for Squawky, not sad for ourselves. This pretty little bird is alive today because you spotted him hanging in the tree. You're a hero, Sally!"

40

That really cheered Sally up.

"Hey, you're right, Daddy. I guess I am a hero!"

Sally's dad always knew how to say the right things.

"Can we keep him for one more night? Please, Daddy?"

"Well, I think that might be a good idea, honey. It's a little chilly tonight, and we want to make sure Squawky is good and strong when we let him go. Okay, we'll let him go tomorrow morning."

That night Sally kept Squawky close to her and thought about how lonely she would be, not getting to take care of him. But it made her happy to think he would be with his family again. She cared about him so much.

"Sweet dreams, little birdie. I love you."

The next day, Sally's dad put the ladder up against the tree. Sally held Squawky close to her, petting his little head. There was quite a bit of racket coming from the top part of the tree.

"Look, Daddy, it's Squawky's family!" Sally said excitedly.

"Sure enough," her dad agreed.

"Looks like they're getting a little anxious to see the little fella again," he said.

43

"Okay, hand Squawky to me, Sally."

Sally kissed Squawky good-bye and handed him gently to her father.

"I'm sure going to miss you," she whispered.

As Sally's dad placed Squawky carefully on a branch near the nest, Squawky's mother and father hopped on to a branch close to their baby and Sally's father. When Sally and her dad looked at Squawky's parents, the mother bird slowly bowed her head and chirped . . .

"Thank you for saving my baby's life and being so gentle and kind to him," spoke the mother bird.

Sally's dad looked startled and said "You're very welcome, Mrs. Blue Jay."

It was the first time they had ever understood each other.

That evening, as Sally and her dad sat on the couch, talking about their adventures with Squawky, they realized something very important. No matter what you are or who you are or what you look like, if we all work together and love one another, we can all learn to understand one another, and that way we can all survive and be happy forever after.

~ The End~

CPSIA information can be obtained at www.ICGtesting.com
Printed in the USA
BVOW10s1331250714

360478BV00005B/22/P